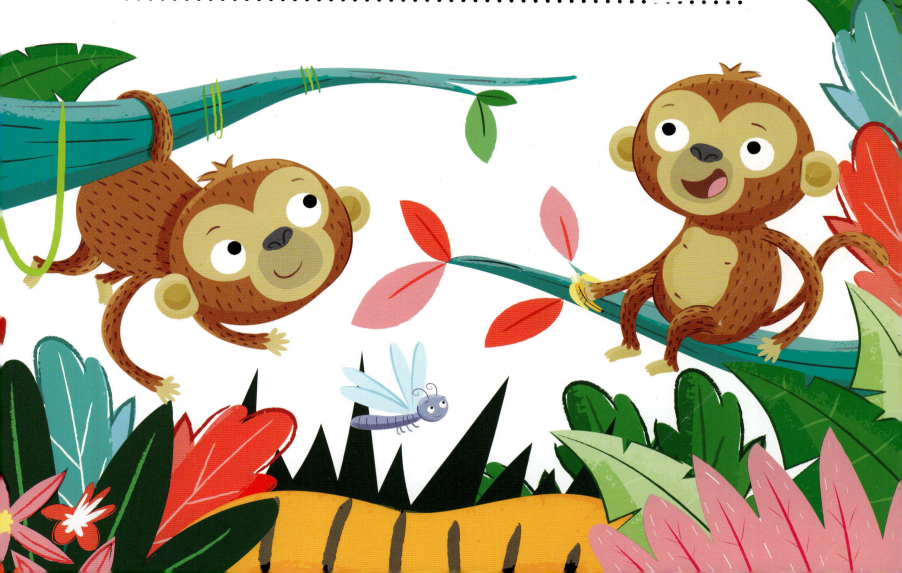

This igloo book belongs to:

....

D0184912

igloobooks

Published in 2016
by Igloo Books Ltd
Cottage Farm
Sywell
NN6 0BJ
www.igloobooks.com

LEO002 0216
2 4 6 8 10 9 7 5 3 1
ISBN: 978-1-78440-420-8

Written by Melanie Joyce
Illustrated by Dean Gray

Designed by Justine Ablett
Edited by Will Putnam

Printed and manufactured in China

Follow That Tiger

igloobooks

Soft, pink nose.

Paws and toes.

Follow Tiger wherever he goes.

Slink, swish, by crocodile.

Hiding in the bush for a while.

He's gone in a **flash**.
Into the water.

Splash!

Legs paddling. Swimming fast.

By the riverbank, at last.

Jump!

Tiger goes up the tree.

Can you see?

Oo-Oo-OO! The monkeys swing away.
They don't want tigers visiting today.

Down comes
Tiger.

Claws
Sharp.

Gripping bark.

He lands on the ground.

Whiskers **twitching.**

Looking around.

Rhino is snoozing.

Hippo, too.

Tiger silently walks on through.

Past the grass and **hissing** snakes.
Not a single noise he makes.

Stripes and stalks seem like one.

Suddenly, Tiger is gone.

Where **IS** he?

Can **you** see?

Wherever could Tiger be?

shh. **Wait.**
Something is coming.

Don't move.

Don't start running.

Can you hear it?

Stay very still.

Be **ever so quiet** until...

...Roar! It's Tiger!

He just likes to say "hi!" when he is passing by.

He wants to know, "What is your name?"
He hopes you've enjoyed his tiger game.